Second Family

Angie Thompson

Quiet Waters Press

Lynchburg, Virginia

Cover design by Angie Thompson
Photo elements by Min An, courtesy of Pexels.com and anatols, licensed through Depositphotos
Sheep logo adapted from original at PublicDomainPictures.net

ISBN: 978-1-951001-00-1 (pbk)
ISBN: 978-0-9996144-9-5 (ePub)

*To anyone who's ever helped a child stay in their home
or offered them a place in yours*

Table of Contents

One

When they paged me to the office that day, family was the last thing on my mind. I'd been a witness to the candy corn incident on the steps that morning, for one thing, and I hadn't been asked yet about what went down between Devlon Burks and Mr. Winchester during P.E. last week. Since our principal knew me from middle school, it wasn't unusual for her to call me for testimony on things like that.

But the first thing I saw was Mikyah Byrd curled in a chair, shaking like January with the windows down instead of October with no A/C. I wanted to run to him, but I forced myself to walk to the desk first and announce myself to the secretary.

"Oh, yes, Jenna." She looked down at her notes. "Your mother said you're to go home with Mikyah. Someone'll pick you both up shortly."

The lady was obviously one of the unconcerned types with the way she squished the name into two syllables with the stress on the "mik." People were always mangling his name like that, like he wasn't worth the trouble to learn to say it right.

"Mi-KY-ah," I corrected her, but if she heard, she didn't answer. I walked over to the row of chairs and put an arm around Mikyah's shoulders. As I'd suspected, his chocolate-milk skin was burning hot. "Finally got it, huh?"

"Thought I was clear." He was talking through clenched teeth, probably to stop them from chattering with the shivers he couldn't control. I gently rubbed his arm, and his head rolled over to rest on my shoulder.

The secretary shot us a pointed look, but I ignored her. I'd started this round of flu, so I wasn't scared of catching it again, and if she was worried about us touching, Mikyah was like a big brother to me, and one day we'd figure out how to make people understand that.

"This leaves who—your mom, my dad, and Davie?"

He didn't answer, just held his breath like he was stifling a groan, and I winced in sympathy. Even my bed hadn't felt soft enough for my bones when I'd been hit with it three weeks ago, and a blue plastic chair and bony shoulder had to be ten times harder. I thought about offering to let him lie down with his head in my lap, but the secretary probably would have blown a fuse. I put my free hand to his forehead instead, as if that would do anything to cool the warmth that radiated through it.

"It'll be all right, Ky," I murmured. "You know the drill. First couple days you just want to curl up and die, and then it gets better. You'll be back at this old place in a week. And don't worry about the kids," I added quickly, knowing what his biggest concern would be. "We'll take care of them—and you—when your mom's not around."

His breath caught sharp for a second before he nodded, and I couldn't tell if it was from pain or something deeper. His mom hadn't been around much the last month or so, but that didn't have to be a bad sign, did it? I didn't like to think bad of people, but I had to admit that Ms. B hadn't done much to justify my optimism.

"Why'd they pull you?" Mikyah murmured, and I caught myself before a shrug that would have jostled his already aching head.

"Obviously because they know I'm the nurse extraordinaire."

Mikyah gave a halfhearted snort that turned into a cough, and I smiled a little as his dark, curly hair brushed my cheek. We'd both done our share of nursing in the last couple weeks as the members of our families passed the bug back and forth. His nine-year-old sister, Amary, had been the last to come down with it and could have gone back to school on Saturday, if they'd had it. We'd all hoped that would be the end of it, but apparently we'd hoped too soon.

I thought of the leaky air mattress on the floor of the tiny room Mikyah shared with his two brothers and

3

winced. He really needed something more comfortable, at least for the duration of the fever. Was there any chance Mom and Dad would agree to drag my mattress next door and let me camp out in a sleeping bag until he was better? They did a lot for Mikyah's family, but dismantling my bed might be over the top. Then again, they knew how much the Byrd kids depended on us. We weren't rich by a long shot, but we weren't nearly as poor as they were— and my parents were a lot better at spending their money carefully than Mikyah's mom.

I wasn't sure how they'd managed until we'd moved in the summer before little Dayzha was born. Mom and Dad hadn't liked the look of the neighborhood, but Mom's medical bills had piled up, and the house we'd been renting got sold, and this apartment was ground floor and near enough to the therapy center that Mom could get there on her own so Dad could work regular hours again.

The Byrd family had been there already—five dirty kids and a pregnant single mom who sometimes yelled loud enough to hear through the walls. We'd done our best to stay away from them for the first few weeks, but then Mikyah had caught Davie about to wander from the playground into the parking lot and come back to settle Amary's hash for the argument with Melissa that'd distracted me. Ever since then, we'd counted the younger children our joint responsibility, and over the next three years, we'd all become the closest of friends. Better than

4

that, my family had invited theirs to church and Mikyah and his mom had given their lives to the Lord. Ms. B still struggled a lot at times, but Mikyah's faith was growing by leaps and bounds, and just last winter he'd led his brother Tyrece, nine at the time, to the Lord as well.

Kids in the neighborhood called us chocolate and vanilla, but Mikyah and I didn't mind, and we'd made it a joke for the younger kids. We were a bit of an odd mix, and we knew it—my family with such pale skin that a summer in the sun baked us to the color of not-quite-done toast and Mikyah's family with skin tones ranging from his creamy brown to little Dayzha's rich dark chocolate. But I didn't care what anyone else said. We really did go well together, just like chocolate and vanilla.

The door to the office opened to the little beeping sound that was more or less annoying than a bell, depending on which you were listening to at the time, and a dark-haired, olive-skinned woman in a classy-looking business suit walked up to the desk and handed her ID to the secretary. I didn't recognize her, so I turned my attention back to Mikyah. He'd stopped shaking so bad, but his eyes were closed and his breathing was heavy.

"Jenna?" My head snapped up, and I found the newcomer standing in front of us. She tilted her head toward the door. "Your mom asked me to bring the two of you home."

I shifted to stand, then paused. I didn't know this woman, and nice clothes didn't equal honesty. What if she'd given the lady at the desk a fake ID or something? No way was I getting in some stranger's car without more proof.

"I need to talk to my mom."

The woman smiled and held out her cell phone, and I ignored the contact she'd pulled up with my mom's name and keyed in the numbers myself. Mom's voice picked up on the second ring.

"Ruth?"

"Mom, it's me."

"Oh, hey, Jen. Soup's in the oven."

I sighed with relief as my lips turned up at Mom's goofy code phrase. But the fact that this lady was legitimate didn't answer all my questions.

"Is something going on? Is everyone okay?"

The silence on the other end held long enough that I knew the answer before Mom spoke.

"Just come with Ruth, sweetheart. I'll fill you in as soon as I can, okay? How's Ky?"

"Pretty terrible. Hey, Mom, can we switch mattresses or something for a couple days? You know how—"

"We can talk about it later, Jenna. Ruth's in a hurry, and she's doing me a favor picking you up. Just come with her and do what she says, okay?"

"Yes, ma'am." A little shiver of cold that had nothing to do with fever snaked its way up my backbone. I ended the call and held the phone out toward Ruth. "Thanks."

"You're a smart girl, Jenna." In a hurry or not, her smile seemed genuine. "Ready to go?"

I nodded and slipped from my chair, then hurried to help Mikyah up and put a steadying arm around his waist. We slowly followed Ruth to her car, leaving the scowling secretary in our wake.

Two

Ruth glanced back at us as she opened the passenger door.

"Mikyah, is it? Why don't you take the front so you can put the seat back? Jenna, do you mind sitting behind me?"

I shook my head and hurried around the car as Mikyah collapsed into the posh leather seat and fumbled with his buckle. Strapping myself into the back, I laid a hand against his forehead again as the seat bent smoothly toward me in response to a button.

"Flu, huh?" Ruth glanced at us in the rearview mirror as she maneuvered into traffic, and I nodded.

"Yep. Most of us already got it. Thought maybe Ky'd escape."

"You two are close?"

I bit my lip to stifle a groan. Were we going to have to go through that again? Why did most of the teens and half the adults we met keep wanting to make our friendship something more than it was?

"We're like second family. All of us. Our whole families, I mean."

"Spend a lot of time together?"

I turned my head to look out the window, not sure where these questions were going but not liking them anyway. Just because Mom trusted this woman to pick us up, it didn't mean she was entitled to every detail of our lives, did it? Did doing what she said mean letting a complete stranger into all our family's business?

"Jenna." Her voice held sympathy, and I looked up to see her watching me in the mirror again. "I don't mean to pry. I went to school with your mom, and your parents have asked for my help with something. I'd really like to get as many people's perspectives on the situation as I can."

Situation? My heart started to pound as possibilities and impossibilities flooded my head. Why would my parents have called someone in from the outside? And to help with what?

"There's no reason to panic, hon." Ruth's voice was soothing, but just her presence was frightening now. "I just want to hear about your families. What you do together. How you get along. That kind of thing."

"We—we live next door." I swallowed hard and glanced toward Mikyah. His eyes were closed, but I thought his face was paler than usual. "We're always—us kids, I mean—it's like one big family. In and out all the time, you know?"

"In and out of both your places?"

That question was a minefield. I knew Mikyah did his best to keep their place livable, but it was never what could really be called clean unless my mom and dad took a hand. But I didn't see how that was any of Ruth's business, and I certainly didn't want to get their family in trouble.

"Mostly our place. Sometimes theirs. We have a three bedroom." That didn't make our living room bigger or change the fact that Mom and Dad didn't like us in anyone's apartment for long without an adult, but hopefully it sounded reasonable.

"Sleep over very often?"

"Not—much." I tried to think back. "Mostly just for emergencies and stuff. Usually it's just, you know, dinner, homework, games, that sort of thing." That was mostly true, although breakfast was becoming more and more common, and "emergencies" had begun to count times when Ms. B was out and the kids were sick and Mikyah was exhausted.

"And you all get along?"

"Definitely." I hoped the confidence in that answer didn't emphasize the hesitation in the others. "I mean, sure, there are arguments and stuff. But yeah. It's like family."

"So you said." A little smile curved the corner of her mouth as she glanced back at me again. "Is that how you feel about it, Mikyah?"

I had to give her points for pronouncing his name right, but I was still annoyed that she'd bother him when he was so obviously miserable. Mikyah gave a weak nod.

"Yeah. Dentons have been real good to us."

"In what way?"

"Letting us hang around. Helping out some." His back arched suddenly, and he clenched his teeth in an obvious spasm of pain before relaxing again with a gasp that turned into a string of coughs. I squeezed his shoulder hard.

"We help out with groceries sometimes. Or, you know, the light bill or something. It costs a lot with so many kids. And sometimes Ms. B can't work all the hours she wants."

I knew it wasn't that simple. Mom had tried over and over to show Ms. B how much better she could do with her food stamps if she'd lay off the snacks and junk food. And I couldn't keep track of how many jobs she'd had—and lost for various reasons—in the three years we'd known her. But I felt Mikyah's shoulder relax a little under my hand, and I knew he appreciated the protection.

"Tell me about the kids."

"Which ones?" I eyed her carefully. Mom and Dad knew Mikyah's biggest fear was that somebody'd decide Ms. B wasn't fit to raise them and stick them in foster care. They wouldn't have called a social worker, would they?

"All of them." Ruth flashed me what seemed to be a sincere smile. "Your mom has how many now—three?"

"Four."

"Are you all the same ages?"

I guessed a rundown of names and ages couldn't hurt. If she was official, she could probably pull all their school records anyway. I shrugged.

"Pretty close. I'm fourteen, and Mikyah's fifteen. We're oldest. My sister Kate's twelve, and Ky's brother Tyrece is ten. Amary and Melissa are both nine. Davie's seven—he's my only brother. Then Shyla's six, Kyron's five, and Dayzha's two."

"That's ten of you altogether?"

"Mm-hmm."

"Sounds like quite a crowd."

"We like it." I straightened my shoulders. "Dayzha's everybody's baby. She's starting to talk in whole sentences now. Tyrece is trying to teach Davie and Kyron to play basketball. Amary and Melissa are pretty much joined at the hip except for about once a week when they decide they won't be friends anymore for an hour or so. And Kate's gotten really good at fixing the little girls' hair. She says it's a lot easier to work with than Melissa's." I swallowed back a wince, hoping Ms. B wouldn't get in trouble for letting someone else do her daughters' tiny braids.

"And what do you and Mikyah do?" Ruth's smile was wider, like she realized she'd finally gotten me to give her more than a guarded listing of facts.

I bit my lips and considered carefully. Mikyah did just about everything for his family except work, drive, and shop. He was the one who tucked the kids in most nights, made sure their homework was done, got them out the door in time for school or church. I'd seen him change diapers, clean up after sick kids, and even cook when there was anything easy in the house. But I couldn't say any of that. I tried to focus on the times we were all together.

"Mikyah's like everybody's big brother. He looks out for us. Watches for ways to help. If anybody's sad or feeling left out, that's where you'll find Mikyah."

"And you?" Ruth asked, and I shook my head.

"I don't do much."

"She reads." Mikyah's hoarse voice cut in before Ruth could respond. "Tells stories. Sings. Great to have around at naptime. Or anytime." A coughing fit cut off anything else he might have planned on saying, and I rubbed his shoulder gently as I looked out at the rush-hour traffic and tried to calculate our distance from home. Ruth gave him a sympathetic smile.

"You two have quite the mutual admiration society. How long have you known each other?"

"About three years," I answered quickly so Mikyah wouldn't have to. "Ever since we moved into Green Hill."

"Planning on staying there a while?"

I sent a quick glance at Mikyah, and his pain-clouded eyes locked on mine. It was something that had always been in the backs of our minds, but we'd agreed long ago not to talk about it. Mom and Dad had never meant to stay in the apartment forever, but the thought of losing the Byrd kids felt like losing a part of myself.

"I don't know," I said slowly. "But if we ever move—well, we'd just have to come back and visit. A lot."

Mikyah pressed his lips together and tried to smile, and I wanted to throw my arms around him and protect him from the world. Was that what this was about? Could Ruth be a realtor? Why would she be asking so many questions about the Byrds, then? Ms. B barely managed the rent on the Green Hill apartment every month, so she'd never be able to move anywhere Mom and Dad were looking. Unless they'd found a big house we could all rent together. My heart gave a wild leap at the thought, but it dropped again at Ruth's next words.

"What about other family, Mikyah? Any relatives you know of besides your mom and siblings?"

Mikyah's hairline was beaded with sweat, and somehow I didn't think it was from the fever.

"Our dads—aren't in the picture. Never have been. Mawmaw—my mom's mom—used to come stay with us sometimes. But she's in a nursing home now. Mom's got a cousin, Calvin, but she doesn't let him around us much."

I remembered their Mawmaw as a tired old lady who'd stayed with the kids for a few months not long after Dayzha was born, when Ms. B was in jail on a drug charge. I'd only seen their cousin Calvin once, but the glimpse I'd had of his eyes had convinced me that I never wanted to see him again. Ruth was silent. Mikyah shifted a little to face her and voiced a question of his own.

"Why?"

"Why what?" Ruth didn't look back at us.

"Why all the questions? What's it matter? Are you a counselor or some—" A heavy bout of coughing cut off Mikyah's words, and I loosened my seatbelt a little and reached over to rub his back. Mikyah groaned but didn't pull away.

Ruth didn't answer for a long minute after Mikyah stopped coughing. I stared at the mirror until she met my eyes with a sigh.

"No, I'm not a counselor."

"Then what are you? Why did Mom and Dad want your help? What's it got to do with the Byrds?" When she didn't answer, my eyes roamed around the car for any trace of a clue. They landed on a parking sticker on the rear window, and I silently read the backwards words "Wright, Meyer & Dunlap." Companies with names like that were usually accountants or— I squinted at the tiny gavel embedded in the logo. "You're a lawyer."

Ruth's eyes snapped back, caught on the parking sticker, and widened in dismay. Mikyah's face had gone the color of Mom's coffee after she drowned it in creamer. He raised himself on his elbow, and his breath came in ragged gasps.

"It's my mom, isn't it? Drugs?"

Ruth glanced at him, then away again.

"Please." Mikyah's voice was hoarse and choked, but I could hear the desperation through the pain. Ruth let out a long sigh.

"Mrs. Denton wanted to tell you herself, but yes."

Mikyah fell back against the seat, wrapping his arms around his chest and burying his face in his shoulder. He was shaking again, but whether it was from fever, pain, or tears, I couldn't tell. Less than a minute before, not knowing what was going on had seemed the worst thing in the world for both of us, but seeing Mikyah hurt like this felt ten times worse. Ruth gave him a minute before she spoke again.

"Did you know?"

Mikyah shook his head, and his forehead creased with pain.

"Wondered. Hoped. She's been clean—two years. I thought maybe—" The words choked off, and he held his breath like he was warding off another cough.

Ruth opened her lips but closed them again without a word. I didn't dare ask what else she'd been about to say. None of us said another word as Ruth pulled onto our street and parked near the building.

17

Three

I was out of my seat like a shot and around the other side to help Mikyah out. He leaned on me harder than he ever had before, and I was sure it had to be from the shock as much as the pain. Ruth rang the bell, and Mom came to open the door, waving for Mikyah and me to follow her in. Mikyah paused on the threshold, looking more than a little lost, and Mom glanced up from where Ruth was speaking in a hurried whisper.

"Come on in, Ky. Do you mind taking the couch? I'd rather not leave you home alone right now."

Mikyah blinked at her as though he couldn't quite believe it, and I pulled him over to the couch, where he flopped with a groan.

"Give me two minutes, Ruth." Mom wheeled her chair into the kitchen and came back quickly with the too-familiar medicine box. "What'd they give you at school, and how long ago?"

"Tylenol. Eleven." Some of the stiffness in his shoulders relaxed at Mom's gentle, efficient tone.

Mom handed him a thermometer and made a note on her little pad. I shoved both our backpacks into the closet and leaned closer to watch the numbers, which stopped at a little over 102. Mom made another note and took the thermometer back, frowning when Mikyah started to cough again.

"Jenna, a glass of water would help." She reached for the cough syrup, and I hurried for the kitchen. When I came back, Mikyah downed the medicine and half the water and dropped back onto the couch pillow, looking miserable and exhausted. Mom started to back away, but Mikyah suddenly raised his head and looked at her with tears in his eyes.

"Nan—" He seemed to catch himself halfway through the nickname Kyron had given my mom years ago and shook his head a bit. "Ms. Maryann, I know you can't do this anymore. But thanks."

"Can't do what, Ky?" Mom didn't comment on the unusual formality as she rolled herself back toward the couch and bent closer to look at him.

"You told Mom—no more drugs. Or you couldn't keep helping us." Mikyah was trembling with the effort it took to stay upright, and I reached to pull his shoulders down, but Mom was there ahead of me.

"Listen close and get this straight, Mikyah. What we said was that we wanted to help your mom get back on her feet, but we couldn't do that unless she gave up the drugs. The fact that she's broken that trust doesn't mean that we love or care about any of you any less. Or that there aren't still things we can do to help. Understand?" She took a deep breath and glanced over her shoulder at Ruth, then back at Mikyah. "I need to go speak to Ruth for a few minutes, and then we'll talk. Okay?"

Mikyah closed his eyes, and Mom nodded at me to stay with him. She motioned for Ruth to follow her into the kitchen, and a few seconds later the back door clicked behind them. I sank to the floor next to the couch and watched Mikyah's uneven breathing and the stiffening of his muscles as the familiar waves of pain rolled over him. Every once in a while he'd brush a sleeve across the corner of his eye, and I wondered why God had let everything fall on him at once like this. It was hard to know exactly what to pray, but I tried, praying for Mikyah, for the other kids, for my parents and whatever it was Ruth was trying to help with, even that Ms. B'd really let God turn her life around this time.

After a while, the back door clicked again, and Dad came out of the kitchen carrying Dayzha. I wondered whether he'd gone to work at all and whether they'd picked Dayzha up from daycare early or just never taken her in. Mom and Ruth followed them out, and Dad put Dayzha in Mom's lap, then headed out the door with Ruth. Mom set Dayzha behind the baby gate in the corner, handed her her favorite tub of dolls and dinosaurs, and came over to the side of the couch. I moved to sit on the end table where I could see her more clearly. She gently brushed a hand across Mikyah's cheek.

"I know it's a bad time, Ky, but we need to talk."

"Yes'm." Mikyah rolled over to face her, trying to stifle a groan.

"Ruth tells me you know your mom's been arrested."

"I've been trying to figure it out." Mikyah shifted and held his breath for a second, coughing a little as he relaxed. "Mawmaw can't come with her hip like it is. Will they have to put us with Calvin? You think there's any way they'd let us stay on our own for a few months—if we had someone, you know, just to look in on us?" He eyed Mom's face like he was afraid that was asking too much. Mom closed her eyes for a second.

"Ky, before you try to make any plans, there's something you need to know."

Mikyah went still as he watched her.

"They didn't arrest your mom on possession." Mom took a deep breath. "They got her on sale."

His face blanched to the color of light wood at the hardware store, the kind that showed green around its edges.

"No." The word was a whisper, and Mikyah buried his face in his hands, hardly seeming to breathe. When he looked up at Mom again after a long minute, his eyes were dull and hollow. "That's her third strike. She'll get—"

"I know." Mom reached for his hand and squeezed it hard. His whole body had gone limp.

"That's it. We're done." His lip trembled, and he bit at it with what seemed his last bit of strength. Mom gently stroked his hair and forehead.

"Don't give up yet, Ky."

"They'll split us up. They'll have to. Nobody'll take six." His breathing suddenly sped up, and his eyes went wide.

"Mikyah." Mom spoke sternly for the first time, but her hand didn't stop its gentle motions. "Lie still and breathe slowly. There's more we need to talk about, but you can't panic. God has this under control. Do you trust Him?"

Mikyah squeezed his eyes shut and fought to slow his breathing. When he lay limp and still again, Mom turned to me.

"Do you understand what's going on, Jenna?"

"Just the part about Ms. B getting arrested. She was selling drugs?"

Mom nodded.

"Having them would be one thing—bad enough but not nearly as serious. This is even worse than usual, though, because she's got a couple bad charges already on her record. Gang-related things from when she was younger. This is her third serious offense, which means she'll get a very strict sentence."

"How strict?" I wouldn't have asked in front of Mikyah, but from his reaction, I guessed he already knew.

"Twenty-five to life."

"Twenty-five years?" I gasped, and Mom's shoulders drooped. She'd tried so hard to help Ms. B. It must be terrible to see everything end like this. I did a couple quick calculations in my head and tried to swallow my shock. If she got the lightest sentence possible, she wouldn't be free until Mikyah was forty and little Dayzha was twenty-seven.

"We'll pray God truly gets hold of her heart. He can do it in prison, you know." Mom moved her hand from Mikyah's hair to softly touch his cheek. He opened his eyes, and the pain in them cut so deep that I had to look away. "Ky, your mom called us this morning. She admits what she did was wrong. Says she got in with a bad crowd in her last job. Thought she'd make some quick money and get out. She knows she's hurt all of you and wants to try to make it right."

"She can't." The dull tone in Mikyah's voice hurt worse than the hoarseness. "I mean, I'll forgive her. I got to. But—she can't fix it."

"No, she can't. But she would like to try to see that you're safe. And together."

Mikyah gave a little huff that was almost a snort, followed by a weak cough.

"No foster place is gonna take six. Not together. Maybe a couple—some of the little ones."

"She's offering to sign over guardianship—even agree to adoption—if we'll take you."

"What?" Mikyah sat up straight on the couch, and Mom eased him back down. I noticed he was starting to shiver again. "That's not fair. She can't do that. You've done—enough—already." Coughs shook his body, and Mom covered him with a light blanket and gently rubbed his back until he was still.

"You're right, Ky. It's a lot for her to ask. But that doesn't necessarily mean it's the wrong thing to do."

I hardly dared to breathe as I waited for her to go on. She glanced up and shook her head a little as she saw my face.

"Ky, I know you're not in the best shape to talk right now, but I really need to hear from both of you. The others will follow your lead. Dad and I have prayed about it and feel a peace about going forward, but that doesn't necessarily mean things will work out. I want you both to know upfront that even if we all decide we want this, it still might not happen."

"You don't have to—" Mikyah started, but Mom cupped his chin and turned it to face her.

"Let's get one thing straight right at the beginning. If we do this, it won't be because we have to, or because of any kind of guilt trip, or because we feel sorry for your mom. It will be because we love each and every one of you, and because we want you in our family, and because we believe it's what's best for us all. We can't go any farther unless you believe that." She held Mikyah's gaze for a long moment, and I saw his shoulders relax as he dipped his head in agreement.

"If this happens, you'll be in the unique position of forming a family with your best friends. In one way, that'll make things easier. In another way, it'll be harder." She glanced up at me as if to be sure I was listening. "We'll all have to rethink our roles a little bit. The Byrd kids are used to 'Denton rules' in spurts, not all the time. You're used to being able to go back home when you get tired of us. Ky, you're used to being in charge in certain ways that might not continue. The Denton kids are going to have to get used to sharing everything, including Dad and me, all the time. You'll have to understand that it'll take time for everyone to settle in, and that it might feel like certain people are getting away with things for a while. You won't be able to play brother or sister when you feel like it and retreat when you don't. Everyone is going to need a whole lot of love and grace. I don't want a fast answer; I want a considered one. Do you think you can do it and set an example for the others?"

I had been nodding my head most of the time she was talking, but now I made myself sit back and think. Mom was right; we'd played at being brothers and sisters for a long time, but this was a whole different level of commitment. I'd been known to send Amary home when she got out of hand, or to hide out in my room so Shyla couldn't beg another story, or to plan projects for times when certain grubby little fingers wouldn't be around. Making the Byrd kids part of our family would change things a lot. Would the trouble be worth it? I lifted my head just as Mikyah's hoarse voice whispered, "We can do it."

"So can we." I reached over and squeezed his arm, and he gave me what was probably meant to be a smile. I could tell he was worn out, and I was sure Mom could, too.

"That's one thing settled, then. Remember, even if everyone agrees, we're still going to have to get court approval, and there are several significant hurdles there."

"Money," Mikyah murmured, and Mom nodded.

"That's one of them. Ruth's agreed to help with the legal paperwork for a very reduced fee, but we're definitely going to need more space—and more food, clothes, a bigger van, you name it. I don't think there's any way we could make it happen on Dad's present salary. But—" She held up a hand before either of us could react. "Dad had an offer for promotion last week.

27

We've been praying about it but didn't feel peace one way or the other. Not until today. The salary would be enough to live on and find a house that would hold all of us. But it would mean moving to Sacramento."

I gulped as I processed this new piece of the puzzle. Moving away from the city I'd spent my whole life in wasn't a little thing. Was I willing to leave everything I knew behind to give us a chance at a new family? But was I willing to lose that family for the sake of everything else I knew? I looked up at Mom with a smile.

"Sounds perfect."

"Anywhere." Mikyah nearly groaned the word, and Mom reached over to smooth his hair again as Dayzha started beating a dinosaur against the wall.

"You get some rest now, Ky. You've had a rough morning. Jenna, would you take Dayzha into your room and try to put her to sleep? I'm going to give Dad a call and then see about some lunch. Are you two hungry?"

"Starving," I answered as Mikyah shook his head. Mom smiled.

"All right, then let's get going. We'll have a lot to plan for this afternoon."

Four

We had barely cleaned up from lunch and started in on making lists when Mom's phone rang. After a rather tense conversation that made no sense from my end, Mom put down the phone and started flipping through folders on the rolling cart we called her desk.

"Something wrong?" I didn't like the set to her jaw or the tight lines in the corners of her mouth.

"Maybe." Mom sighed deeply. "Social worker just showed up at the elementary school."

My heart skipped a beat.

"They can't take them, can they? Ms. B gave them to us."

"Nothing's official yet, Jenna." Mom grabbed two folders and stuffed them into her bag. "I'm going to call Ruth and see if she'll meet me there. Maybe ask Dad to pick Kate up. There won't be room in the minivan, but I'd rather have all of you together right now. Of course no one's going to do anything to Kate. Call it mother hen wanting all the chicks under her wing. Watch Dayzha while I'm gone, please, and keep an eye on Ky. He can have more Tylenol in about an hour if I'm not back. And Jenna?" She waited until I met her gaze. "Don't open the door to anyone until I get back, unless it's Dad or Ruth. Okay?"

I nodded, probably a little longer than I needed to.

"Is there anything else I can do?"

"This would be an excellent time to pray that God's will and only His will be done." Mom came back long enough to squeeze my hand, then she disappeared out the door.

I locked it behind her, then went to check that the back door was locked as well. As I started for the living room again, I stopped to check the kitchen window and tried to laugh at myself. No one was going to force their way in through a window to drag Mikyah and Dayzha away. In my head, I knew that. But something still propelled me down the hallway to check the bedrooms, too. After double-checking all the locks in the living room, I sat down on a chair near Mikyah and tried to settle my suddenly racing heartbeat.

Pray, Mom had said, and I did for a long time as I sat there, tensed and waiting for I wasn't sure what. The clock above the door seemed to crawl. Had Mom even made it to the school yet? Would they let her bring the kids back? Would they come with her to see the apartment? I jumped up and scoured the living room, picking up a stray pencil lying on the bookcase, a doll Dayzha had thrown under a shelf. The floor could have used vacuuming, but that wouldn't have been fair to Mikyah, fast asleep on the couch. I pulled a load of clean laundry from the dryer instead, then scrambled to get it folded as I wondered if I should have left it tucked out of sight. I'd just finished putting the last pieces away and sat down to calm my nerves again when Mikyah rolled over with a deep groan.

"How you feeling?" I looked him over anxiously. He still appeared miserable, but not as pale and exhausted as he'd seemed earlier.

"Like I got run over by a dozen trucks. On an aircraft carrier." Mikyah started to cough, and I hurried for a fresh glass of water.

"Sounds about par for the course. Not sure any of us got the cough this bad, though." I handed him the water, and he took it gratefully, downing most of it in one gulp.

"At least I'm original. Where's your mom?"

I froze as I debated whether to tell him before realizing that my silence had already spoken volumes.

"Social worker showed up at the school."

"Oh, no." He put a hand over his face, and I sat down on the floor next to him and squeezed his arm.

"It'll be okay. Mom called Ruth. She said just wait and pray."

"Funny how fast she went from public enemy number one to champion of justice, huh?"

"Who, Mom?"

"Ruth."

"Oh." I thought back and shook my head. "Was that just a couple hours ago? I guess I was sort of rude, wasn't I?"

"We didn't know what she was after. Makes more sense now." Mikyah shifted and groaned.

"Want to put in a movie or something to take your mind off it?"

"Not yet." He coughed and tried to push himself up against the pillows. I shifted them to support him better, and he closed his eyes. "Unless you've got any long, boring documentaries that'll put me to sleep for a week."

"Afraid we're more musical comedy people." I skimmed the titles on the shelf in front of me and fished one out, grinning. "Strawberry Shortcake?"

"You're cruel."

"Get used to it. You just might have a lot more years with me." I was reaching to put the movie back in place again when Mikyah's quiet voice stopped me.

"Jenna?" When I turned to look, he was watching me with a worried expression. "You're really sure?"

"Of course I am. Why wouldn't I be?"

"Just seems like we're getting everything. Perfect parents. Perfect family. Perfect life. What are you getting? A bunch of rowdy, needy kids with a mom in jail. Doesn't balance."

I knelt to look him directly in the eye.

"First off, if you think we're perfect, you're gonna learn better fast. Like the first time Mom has you watch Davie at the sink to make sure he's actually brushing his teeth, not scrubbing the brush against the faucet and calling it done. And don't think he doesn't do it on purpose. Or when Dad snaps and sends us all to our rooms because a couple of us can't stop arguing. Plus, you already know Mom needs help sometimes with stuff she can't do from her wheelchair. We still buy lots of our clothes from Goodwill, and we'll probably never see Disneyland. But let me tell you what I'm getting. I'm getting the older brother I always dreamed of. I'm getting my best friend who I dreaded leaving as a permanent part of my life. I'm getting a new batch of little brothers and sisters that I already love to death. God brought us together. He wants you to have us and us to have you. It balances just fine."

Mikyah drew a shaky breath, and his chin quivered.

"You're awesome, Jenna."

"You're awesome yourself, Ky. Hey, and maybe pretty soon we can get everybody who keeps wanting to make us an item off our backs once and for all."

Mikyah managed a weak chuckle that brought on another coughing fit. I handed him the rest of the water, and he gulped it gratefully.

"It's books and movies that's the problem, you know," he whispered as he handed back the empty glass. "Anytime people say 'just friends,' it never ends up like that." A small cough seemed to completely drain his lungs, and

33

it took longer than it should have for him to draw a deep breath again.

"You should stop talking." I reached over and pulled the blanket straight where it had fallen off his legs. "And yeah, I know. That's why I need you for a real brother. Then nobody gets to say a word."

Mikyah opened his mouth, then changed his mind and squeezed my hand instead.

"I guess this'll make us chocolate and vanilla family." I grinned as I squeezed back. "All we need's an Irish setter, and we'd be neapolitan."

He murmured something I didn't quite catch, but the words "sun too long" gave me the jist of it. I almost slapped his shoulder but thought better of it in time.

"I told you to stop talking. And it's not our fault we got the gene that burns to a crisp. As a member of this family, you'll get very well acquainted with the sunscreen and aloe bottles. Trust me, they'll be your friends no matter how disgustingly well you tan."

Mikyah gave me a weak grin, and his hold on my hand relaxed. I squeezed one more time, then slipped my hand away and stood.

"You should try to get some more rest. Mind if I vacuum real quick while you're awake?"

He shook his head, then shot a quizzical glance toward the bedroom. I sighed.

"Right. Dayzha. I forgot about that. How come you can remember everything, even when you're sick? No, wait. Don't answer that. Because you're superbrother, that's why. Well, I may not have all your instincts, but I'll try to hold down the fort while you get over this attack of kryptonite. Just leave it to me."

Mikyah managed a half-hearted roll of his eyes before they closed again.

Five

I tiptoed down the hall to check on Dayzha, who was still curled up in the corner of the playpen, then glanced in Davie's room and swept the clothes from the floor into the laundry basket, grateful that Mom had made him clean it up on Saturday. Just as I reached the living room again, something rattled in the lock, and I froze. A second later, Dad appeared with Kate behind him looking as serious and half-scared as I felt. I threw myself into Dad's arms, and he held on tight for a second.

"Hey, baby. Everything's okay. Mom and Ruth are on their way."

"With the kids?"

"Yep. I've told Kate what's going on. I assume you already know."

"Mom talked to us. Is the—is anyone else coming?"

"Yeah, we're going to have company. How's the house look?"

"Pretty good. Dayzha's asleep, so I can't vacuum."

"All right. Let me go get out of my jacket." He glanced over my shoulder at the couch. "How you feeling, Ky?"

It was hard to tell if the answering sound was more a moan or a grunt. I shook my head.

"He's got a bad cough, so he's not supposed to be talking," I answered for him. "Aside from that, he feels about like the rest of us have."

"Which, according to your mom, can be best described as death warmed over with a gelpack."

I hadn't heard Mom say that, but it sounded pretty accurate to me. From the grin that touched the corners of Mikyah's mouth, he agreed.

"That doesn't even make sense." Kate, ever the literal one, wrinkled her forehead in confusion as she stared at Dad. He winked at me and headed for the bedroom.

"The expression's supposed to be 'death warmed over,'" I explained. "But you know how this thing feels. When you're in the middle of it, even that sounds too good for what you're feeling. And a gelpack keeps things warm, but it doesn't warm them up much. So it's like, obviously a little better than death, but just barely."

Kate didn't look convinced, but she shrugged it off and looked down at Mikyah for a minute, then glanced back up at me.

"So, Ms. B said we can have them? All of them?"

"If the judges and everyone say it's okay."

"Where's everybody going to sleep?"

"We haven't figured that out yet. We can squeeze everyone in somewhere. We'll need a new house pretty soon, though."

"Dad told me about Sacramento." Kate nodded and looked up at me with her big eyes that seemed to take everything in. "Are you happy?"

"Not about what happened with Ms. B. But about making them part of our family? Yeah. I am."

Kate nodded again, but she still looked serious.

"You think they'll let us?"

"I don't know. I hope so."

"Me too." Kate straightened her shoulders. "Dad says Mom's telling the other kids that they're staying with us for now, but not that we might be keeping them yet. They don't want to get their hopes up if it doesn't work. He wants us older ones to be careful what we say."

She glanced over at Mikyah, who gave a faint nod, and I smiled. Letting Kate in on what "the older ones" were doing was always the best way to get her help with anything. When she turned back to me, I nodded solemnly.

"So what are we supposed to do when that lady gets here?" Kate's forehead puckered, and I thought quickly.

"Act polite. Be on your best behavior. We can't just go up to her and say, 'Back off; we can handle this,' but we've got to show her we can. She needs to see that we all like each other and that we listen and obey Mom and Dad."

"That's right." I hadn't seen Dad in the hall until he stepped forward. "And that doesn't mean cookies and angel smiles, Kate. She'll see right through that. We need real good, not fake good, okay? So help where you can, but don't get in the way, and watch the arguments and the bossing—even when you're sure you're right." He tugged lightly on one of Kate's braids and pulled her into a quick side hug.

A car door snapped shut outside, and I turned to peer through the blinds. A young lady with curly blond hair pulled back into a severe ponytail was striding purposefully toward our end of the building.

"I think she's here." I glanced down at the unvacuumed carpet and winced. Dad squeezed my shoulder.

"It's been a busy morning, Jenna, and we've got a sleeping toddler. She can't expect perfection."

An extra-loud clang of the doorbell echoed through the house, and I winced.

"Not sure how long she'll stay sleeping." I glanced toward the couch to see Mikyah struggling to a sitting position, but as I reached out to stop him, Dad spoke quickly.

"Stay right where you are, Ky. You don't have to impress anyone. If she's never seen a case of the flu before, she'll get used to it fast. You rest and leave this to us, understand?"

The worry didn't leave Mikyah's face, but he let me pull him back down to the pillows. From the way he trembled, I didn't think he'd have had the strength to stay upright more than a few minutes if he'd wanted to. I wasn't sure if sitting on the end table would be a point against us, so I sat on the floor next to the couch instead. Kate scooted closer and took the end of the loveseat next to me as Dad opened the door.

"Can I help you?" I wasn't sure how Dad managed to keep his voice so normal. Looking down at my hands, I found they were trembling almost as bad as Mikyah's and quickly shoved them behind my back.

"I'm looking for David Denton." The young woman's voice was crisp and professional, but it had an edge to it that I didn't like.

"You're speaking to him."

"I understand that you have the children of"—the woman glanced quickly down at her clipboard—"Annetta Byrd living in your home?"

"There are only two of them here at the moment." Dad's tone didn't change, but he didn't move out of the doorway.

"Your wife hasn't returned with the other children yet?" Even from a distance and over Dad's shoulder, I could see the woman's eyebrow go up.

"Miss—" Dad paused deliberately. "Excuse me, I didn't catch your name."

Everyone knew that was because she hadn't offered it, but I was proud of the way Dad managed to put both authority and politeness in his tone.

"Chelsea. Lauren Chelsea. I'm with the child welfare office. I spoke with your wife at Deer Point Elementary, and she assured me she would bring the children here immediately."

"Miss Chelsea." Dad's voice held a trace of humor. "Do you have any idea how long it takes to gather six children and load them into the car?"

"Six?" Miss Chelsea leaned forward like a bulldog on a scent. "I was informed there were only four children enrolled at Deer Point."

"Four of the Byrd children and two of my own."

"And why are your children being removed early?"

"Because we would rather spare them the fear of discovering that the friends they rode in to school with are not on the bus coming back."

I wasn't sure how Dad could be so polite when every question from the woman's mouth felt like an accusation. She apparently didn't have an answer for his last statement and jumped back to an earlier one.

"You stated there are two of the Byrd children in your home at the moment."

"That's correct. Mikyah and Dayzha."

"And why is"—she glanced down at her clipboard again—"Mikyah not in school?"

I had to stop myself from groaning out loud. She'd put in all three syllables but pronounced the middle one "key" like something you'd use in a lock. And while she hadn't sounded overly confident, the blatant change from what Dad had just said made it obvious that she didn't trust him to know any of the correct pronunciations.

"He was." Dad's tone was still amazingly unruffled. "We got a call from the school at eleven this morning asking us to pick him up because he'd come down with the flu."

"Flu?" Miss Chelsea cocked her head as if there was something unusual about that.

"Yes. It's been going around the family for a couple weeks."

"And has he been tested to verify that it is indeed a case of the flu?"

"Miss Chelsea." Dad sighed for the first time. "As I told you, we received the call at eleven this morning. It's not yet three in the afternoon. Knowing the circumstances, you may imagine how busy we've been in those intervening hours. We haven't yet made it to the doctor for an official diagnosis, but his symptoms closely match those of his siblings and members of my family who have recently had bouts of the flu."

"Mr. Denton." Miss Chelsea's voice was crisper than ever. "I gather from speaking to your lawyer that you are aware of the nature of the charges against Annetta Byrd?"

The sour way she said "your lawyer" made me cover a smile and give Ruth a mental thumbs-up.

"I am," Dad agreed without emotion.

"And yet when her son exhibits suspicious symptoms at school, you don't think it prudent to have them investigated immediately?"

Behind me, Mikyah gave a sharp gasp. I was still trying to figure out what she meant when Dad's answer made it clear.

"Miss Chelsea, if you're suspecting that Mikyah's illness is in any way drug-related, I can assure you, you are mistaken. If necessary, we'll take him in for an official diagnosis, but there is nothing in the least suspicious about his symptoms. I'm sure the school nurse will agree, if you care to consult her. She would have filed a report if anything unusual was suspected, wouldn't she?"

"Nurses are not infallible, Mr. Denton."

"No, they are not, Miss Chelsea. May I ask if you have any medical background?"

The woman seemed confused for a moment.

"Well, I have taken a few courses—on several medical topics. Why is that relevant?"

"Because you seem determined to offer a diagnosis on Mikyah without having examined him or gathered knowledge of any of his symptoms beyond the fact that they are flu-like. I doubt that any medical professional would venture to offer an opinion based on such incomplete information."

Kate gave me an open-mouthed stare and quickly moved one finger as though notching a point for Dad. I pursed my lips and shook my head, trying to keep from smiling. Dad was doing a great job, but getting smug and cocky wasn't going to help our case any.

"I would like to come in and see the children, Mr. Denton." Miss Chelsea's tone was showing definite frustration now.

"And you may, Miss Chelsea, as soon as my wife and Mrs. Meyer arrive."

Kate tapped my shoulder and mouthed, "Who?" I started to shrug, but then it clicked, and I leaned over to whisper, "Probably Ruth. She's a lawyer."

Miss Chelsea peered over Dad's shoulder and seemed to see Kate and me for the first time.

"And were your older children also afraid to ride the bus alone today?"

The sarcasm in the question was evident, and Kate stiffened. I put a hand on her knee before she could blurt out something about riding the bus alone every day.

"My older children needed to be involved in some important decision making. They don't make a habit of leaving school early. You may check their attendance records if you'd like to verify that."

Anything Miss Chelsea would have answered was left unsaid as she turned away from the door to watch something in the parking lot. Car doors slammed, and a swirl of voices outside the window told me Mom was home even before Kate's whispered announcement.

Six

Dad bent down to catch Kyron and Shyla as they came barreling through the door.

"Sh-shh. Naptime rules 'til Dayzha wakes up, okay? Where do your backpacks go?"

"By the table," they chorused, along with Davie, who'd also run into the blockade. Dad put a finger to his lips, and they repeated it in a whisper.

"Hey, you guys, bring your library books to me," Kate offered suddenly, moving over to the middle of the loveseat and shoving back the pillows to make room. The three youngest beamed and rushed to dump their things in the kitchen before scurrying back to Kate with a pile of books each.

"Thank you," I mouthed over their heads, and Kate grinned. I wasn't sure how she'd guessed that our usual naptime storytime would have driven me to distraction today, but she'd chosen a great way to help.

Amary and Melissa followed the little ones in, stowed their backpacks, and brought books to Dayzha's corner, but they didn't open them and just sat whispering to each other, much more subdued than usual. Tyrece shuffled in with his head down and didn't even make it to the kitchen before his eyes caught Mikyah. I scooted out of the way just in time as Tyrece flung himself to his knees in front of the couch, burying his head in his brother's shoulder. Mikyah raised himself on one elbow and wrapped his other arm around Tyrece, holding on as tight as he could.

"It'll be okay, Rece," he whispered hoarsely. "God's taking care of us. It'll all be okay."

Tyrece's shoulders shook, and he tightened his grip until Mikyah started to cough. Then he let go but curled up close to the couch, as though not wanting to let Mikyah out of his reach. I understood a little of how he felt. Kyron looked up and slid down from Kate's lap.

"Ky sick?" he asked, edging past Tyrece to look at Mikyah.

"Yeah, like you were, remember? When you got to lay in bed all day and eat popsicles?" I chucked his chin, wanting to get the worry out of his eyes. His face brightened.

"Did Ky get popsicles?"

"Not yet."

"Can I get him one?" He took a step toward the kitchen, but I pulled him back. Dealing with sticky, dripping popsicles did not sound like a social-worker-friendly activity.

"Not right now, Ronny. Maybe later."

Kyron frowned in thought for a moment before looking up again.

"Can I make him a picture?"

"Sure. He'd like that."

Kyron pulled a large book from the shelves, and I grabbed the box of paper and crayons from the top of the bookcase. Shyla's eyes lit up, and she scrambled out from under Kate's arm.

"I wanna draw!"

I put my finger to my lips and nodded at her, and Davie promptly abandoned Kate and the book, declaring that he wanted to cut. I glanced over at Mom and Dad, but they were listening to something Ruth was saying to Miss Chelsea, so I nodded a bit reluctantly and handed Davie a pair of safety scissors. Shyla left her crayons, declaring that she wanted to cut too, and I gave her another pair of scissors and handed them a basket for their scraps. Kate gave me a helpless shrug, and I grinned ruefully and helped her stack the books on the table. Kate settled herself on the carpet and started picking up Shyla's scattered crayons, and I moved over to the corner where Amary and Melissa sat with their backs to the room, still much too quiet.

It wasn't until I was right beside them that I heard a soft sniff, and bending down for a closer look, I saw tear streaks on Melissa's cheeks and a wet patch on her t-shirt where Amary's head rested. Not knowing what else to do, I put my arms around their shoulders, and both girls turned and buried their faces in my chest, their fine gold and coarse dark hair mingling together in a tangled mess that was somehow strangely beautiful. Their sobs were audible now, and I held them close, knowing I couldn't give them the grain of hope I clung to, but hoping that my wordless comfort would somehow help.

Mikyah raised his head as their crying increased in volume and pitch, but when he saw that I had them, he laid back down with a weak nod. Kyron's lip was trembling like he was about to join the party. I tightened my hold and spoke softly but firmly.

"Shh, girls. Everything's going to be okay. Shhh. It's okay to cry, but you'll wake—" I winced as a wail from the bedroom proved my warning too late. "Dayzha."

Instantly both girls were on their feet, gulping back their sobs and drying their tears.

"Can we get her up?"

"Can we?"

I glanced over at Mom, who nodded and smiled as the girls hurried down the hall. In a few minutes they were back with Dayzha toddling between them and holding a hand of each. Melissa carried a clean diaper, and Amary held a pack of wipes, which they dropped in front of me.

"Thanks, girls." I gave them a wry smile, and they giggled as I scooped up Dayzha and her things and carried them toward the kitchen.

"Dink?" Dayzha reached for the faucet as we passed it, and I shook my head.

"In a minute, Zhazha. I need to change you first."

"Dink now!" Her little mouth pulled into an ominous pout, and I froze. I knew very well what the rules on tantrums were and that Dayzha needed consistency and limits from us, now more than ever. But the thought of Miss Chelsea in the other room hearing everything and with the power to take the kids away and stick them in foster care scared me to the core. Which would she think was worse, giving in to Dayzha's demands or standing my ground and letting her scream?

"Need help, Jenna?" Mom's soft voice from the doorway gave me the direction I needed. Mom always did what she believed was right, no matter who was watching. I took a deep breath and focused on Dayzha again.

"Dayzha can have a drink as soon as I change her diaper," I told the little girl firmly, laying her on the floor and catching her legs as she began to kick.

"No! Nan-nan!" She thrust her arms out toward Mom as though pleading for release from torture, and I felt her lungs filling for what was sure to be an ear-piercing wail.

"What color sippy does Dayzha want?" Mom asked, and I breathed a sigh of relief as Dayzha went still to consider the question. The ploy didn't always work, and I sometimes forgot to try it, but this time the little girl let herself be redirected without a fuss. I focused on changing her as fast as I could.

"Byue—wed—yeyyow tippy. Zaza yeyyow tippy!" Dayzha threw her arms in the air like she was cheering a

51

touchdown, and I smiled at her insistence on naming all the color options before she picked one. Mikyah and I were learning to give her time to name everything before forcing her to make a decision—even if it was a choice between two equally pink hairbows. Without warning, the little girl started to sit up, and I barely caught her in time. She reached her hands out toward Mom again. "Nan-nan tick? Zaza help?"

"Yes, as soon as Jenna's done changing you, Zhazha can help with the stick." Mom's smile included me, and I let my shoulders relax as I fastened the clean diaper, pulled up the little jeans, and placed the now grinning toddler on Mom's lap. Dayzha put her hand over Mom's and "helped" guide the reaching stick to the bin of sippy cups on the top shelf. I finished cleaning up as Mom found and filled a yellow cup, then wheeled herself back to the living room with Dayzha on her lap, contentedly sucking on her water.

Seven

"Okay, everyone, let's hit the books," Mom was saying as I re-entered the living room. "If you all get your homework done early, we might be able to make it a movie night. Let's get Shyla, Ron, Davie, and Kate at the table and Amary, Melissa, Rece, and Jenna on the floor. But girls, if you talk, I'm going to make one of you switch. Understand?"

Amary and Melissa grimaced at each other but didn't protest as they hurried for their bags. Kate looked immensely pleased at being placed in charge of the younger kids, even if it was just while Mikyah was sick. Mom spoke softly to Tyrece for a minute, then retrieved a baby word book from one of the low shelves and settled herself near the door with Dayzha. Tyrece rubbed a sleeve across his eyes and pulled a crumpled mess of papers from his backpack. I retrieved my own backpack from the closet, settled myself near the kitchen door, and opened my science book.

"It's absolutely appalling!" Miss Chelsea's voice from the hall arrested me before I was two paragraphs in. "Ten children in this apartment? Why, there's barely space to walk in this room with the playpen up!"

"This is a temporary situation, Miss Chelsea. As we told you, we will be moving soon. I agree, it's crowded, but—"

"Crowded is not the word for it, Mr. Denton!" Miss Chelsea made no effort to lower her voice as she, Dad, and Ruth came down the hallway. "Why, there's not even room at the table for all of them. Where do you expect them to eat?"

"Ooh, can we have a picnic, Nan-nan?" Amary's head popped up from behind the book that was crowded suspiciously close to Melissa's. Miss Chelsea frowned disapprovingly, and Mom sighed a little as she glanced toward the girls.

"Maybe. Homework first. Are you two reading or talking? Do I need to call Davie out?"

Amary shook her head and buried her face in her book again.

"This is entirely unacceptable. It is obviously impossible to keep any kind of order or degree of cleanliness with this many children underfoot." Miss Chelsea's gaze swept from the still-unvacuumed hallway to the crayons and paper scraps left over from the youngest children's art projects. My cheeks flushed with shame, but I had a sudden urge to grab Mikyah's key and let her see just how much dirtier an apartment could be. I put my head down on my book and prayed for God to help me keep a grip on my anger.

"No one believes this is the perfect solution." Ruth's voice was cool and professional, but it didn't carry any of the bite of the social worker's. "But surely leaving them in an environment where they feel safe and with people they trust is preferable to adding to their trauma by splitting them into unfamiliar homes, at least until the court decides on a permanent placement."

"This environment is utterly unsafe!" Miss Chelsea hissed. If she could have melted Ruth with a glare, I was pretty sure she would have done it. "It's against all standards to crush this many children into an apartment this small. And with a wheelchair in the mix!"

"Mrs. Denton's wheelchair doesn't have any bearing on her fitness as a mother." Ruth's tone was a warning, and Miss Chelsea's glare intensified.

"She may be very well equipped to handle her own children." Her tone expressed more doubt than her words. "But that doesn't mean all relevant factors shouldn't be considered when placing other children in the home. Mrs. Denton certainly has the right to apply for custody, if she so desires, but I believe the children's best interests would be served by temporary placements elsewhere until the courts can determine a satisfactory solution."

"And I don't believe you have sufficient grounds to remove them from a home where they are obviously cared for and thriving if your objections are the parent's physical disability and some paper scraps on the floor." I felt a surge of gratitude at Ruth's staunch defense, but Miss Chelsea looked ready to stamp her foot in irritation.

"You can't say you think this apartment is large enough to house twelve people!"

"Under ordinary circumstances, no. But as an emergency measure to keep the children together and with a caregiver they trust? I think the children's welfare is more important than the space limitations."

"The children's welfare is my primary consideration!" Miss Chelsea's voice was rising again, regardless of the little ears pricked toward her. "And I insist that they be moved to a safe and healthy environment immediately!"

"We have a signed statement by Ms. Byrd announcing her intention to sign over her parental rights to the Dentons and her wish that the children remain with them until the paperwork is finalized. As the Dentons have no objection and it's quite usual for children to be placed with friends of the family pending a decision by the courts, I see no legal grounds for you to remove the children from this home."

"You are determined to make this difficult, Mrs. Meyer."

"I am determined to protect my clients and the children in their care, Miss Chelsea."

Miss Chelsea glared at Ruth for several long seconds before turning back to the hallway.

"Very well, since you give me no option, I will inform my supervisor of the situation. You will wish you had done this the easy way." She stalked to the back of the hallway and whipped out her cell phone. Dad shot Ruth a worried glance, and Ruth shook her head slightly. They moved a bit further from the hallway, probably forgetting that they were also moving closer to me.

"Can she take them?" I didn't like the worried crease in Dad's forehead as he asked the question.

"I don't know." Ruth shook her head. "The space issue is a serious one, but I think it could be overlooked as a temporary emergency measure. Who actually has custody over the children is the sticky point. If they're officially in your care, there would have to be a court order to remove them. If child welfare has temporary custody, we're in trouble."

"So which is it?"

"It's an unusual situation, and I don't know all the finer points of the law—if there even is a law. I think our case is strong, and I'm not backing down until I have to. Her other arguments are ridiculous, but the supervisor may have enough clout or legal finesse to override my objections. What I am sure of is that once they're taken away, it becomes much more difficult to get them back. Not to mention, you'll be trying to deal with it from Sacramento, and we lose the argument of familiar environment, same schools, etc."

"Nan-nan, what's this say?" Kyron dashed out of the kitchen and past Dad and Ruth to Mom, handing up a paper, and a smile quirked the corner of Ruth's mouth.

"That is our best argument, and I only hope the supervisor will recognize it."

"Ronny, I can help you!" Kate called from the kitchen, sounding a little frustrated. Kyron finished listening to Mom's explanation and trudged back to his seat, and Dad went over to talk with Mom. Ruth glanced at me, and I put my book down and stood up, feeling like it was no use to even pretend to study right now.

"So, I'm curious." Ruth's tone was back to the polite, inquisitive one she'd used that morning, and I braced myself. "Why is Ky short for Mikyah and not Kyron?"

I laughed at the release of tension and suddenly felt on the verge of tears.

"Because Mikyah had it first. And also Ky's stressed in Mikyah, but Ron's stressed in Kyron. Like Tyrece is Rece and not Ty. Good thing, too, if you're calling across the playground or something. It's tricky with Shyla sometimes, but the soft sound at the beginning makes it easier." I was rambling, and I knew it. The stress was wearing on me more than I'd realized, but Ruth didn't seem to mind. I wondered if maybe she'd asked on purpose to give me some kind of relief. If she had, though, it was short-lived, as the tension returned the moment Miss Chelsea strode down the hall.

"My supervisor is on her way. Unless you would rather make this easier on yourself and your clients and allow me to take the children now."

"I would rather do what is right than what is easy, Miss Chelsea." Ruth gave my arm a quick squeeze and moved over to sit on the loveseat next to Mom. Dad offered one of the kitchen chairs to Miss Chelsea, but she refused and began pacing the entryway.

I let Ruth's words settle a little as I sank back down against the wall and motioned to Melissa, who was tilting her head at her book in the way that meant she'd given up trying to understand it. Nothing about this situation was easy, and maybe it would only get harder from here, but we were doing what was right, and that was what was important. Now if only God would work for us.

Eight

The minutes seemed to crawl by as we waited for the supervisor. I gave up my homework as a lost cause and picked up the worst of the crayon and paper mess. Tyrece blinked at his books with apparently unseeing eyes. Kyron and Shyla finished their work and promptly dumped the crayons again. Dayzha demanded "taurs" and proceeded to make her largest T-rex attack Mikyah until Tyrece chased her off with a pathetically small stegosaur and began playing dino fights with her. Amary and Melissa were caught whispering under cover of the noise and banished to the kitchen with Kate. Davie announced himself done and joined in the dino fight with a loud roar and an unprecedented attack on the helpless doll population.

"Eat doyyie!" Dayzha shrieked, but as I hurried to ward off disaster, she stuffed one of the smallest dolls into the gaping mouth of an angry raptor. I groaned.

"Davie, look what you're teaching Dayzha! Dinosaurs don't attack people; they're all dead." I ignored the whisper in my mind that said they probably had attacked anything and everything, including people, when they were alive. It wasn't the time to debate natural history; my goal was to prevent present carnage.

"Yeah, they do! In Jurassic—"

I cut him off with a loud groan.

"You haven't even seen those movies. How do you even know about them?"

"Oh, Tony and Grant were telling me!" Davie's eyes lit with excitement, and I wondered desperately what parents in their right minds would have put something like that in front of seven-year-olds. "They said there's this one scene where a lady—"

"Stop!" I put up my hand. "I don't want to know, you don't need to know, and Dayzha definitely doesn't. Make them eat just each other for now, okay?"

I didn't wait for his agreement but quickly scooped the dolls back into the bin and shoved it onto its shelf. Dayzha pouted for a second, then turned the raptor on Davie's arm instead, and he went down on the floor with sound effects suggesting a gruesome death and Dayzha giggling uproariously, while Tyrece's tiny stegosaur snapped at his head and Kyron abandoned his crayons to join the fray.

"Jenna." Mom's voice stopped me from burying my face in my hands, and I hurried over to the kitchen door, wondering why I hadn't noticed when she'd left Ruth. "They're fine. This is boy play. Just let them get their energy out."

"But Dayzha—"

"Has three older brothers. It's okay. There are limits, even to boy play, but you can let this go. Would you take Ky's temperature again and then give him these?"

She handed me two Tylenol and a dose of cough syrup, and I balanced them carefully with the thermometer and the water glass as I stepped around crayons, dinosaurs, and little boys who were dying and reviving at an incredible rate. Dayzha didn't seem to have caught on to the dying part of the game, and every time one of their dinosaurs snapped at her, she would just duck away with a squeal before returning to snap with her own dinosaur and giggle as her victim flopped on the floor again. I eased myself onto the edge of the couch next to Mikyah, who barely stirred.

"Time for more medicine, Ky. Mom wants your temperature first, though."

He acknowledged me with a weak moan and didn't turn his head, but when I set the water on the table and slipped the thermometer between his lips, he reached a shaking hand up to hold it. His fever had climbed a little higher than last time, and I hoped the medicine would help to knock it down. At first glance, his breathing seemed easier, until I noticed that he was only taking quick breaths that barely moved his chest.

"You shouldn't be breathing like that, Ky. You're not half filling your lungs. You'll hyperventilate or something."

"Hurts. Makes me cough." He proved his point with a coughing fit that shook his entire frame. I held the cough syrup to his lips and reached for the water.

"This should help. But try to breathe deep anyway, okay? Just another day or so of the bad stuff, and then you'll start feeling a lot better. I promise." I waited until he had downed all the medicine and most of the water before continuing. "I'm sorry there's not a quieter place. Maybe you could move into Davie's room. I can ask Mom."

Mikyah shook his head with an effort.

"It's fine. You're doing—everything—" Another coughing spell cut him off, and I gave him the rest of the water, squeezed his shoulder, and went to refill the empty glass and drop the medicine cup in the sink. On second thought, I pulled it back out, washed it, and set it in the dishrack before returning to leave the water on the table again. Hurrying back to Mom's side, I reported Mikyah's temperature, and she noted it on her little pad.

"How's he doing?"

I shook my head.

"About like I felt. Really weak and listless. Except his cough's really bad. He says breathing deep makes it worse."

Mom frowned and glanced toward the couch, but before she could make a move toward Mikyah, there was a knock at the front door. Mom handed me the medicine box and moved toward the door with Dad as Ruth got to her feet and Miss Chelsea reached for the knob. When I returned from the kitchen after helping Kate explain a fraction worksheet to Amary, all the adults were deep in conversation with a tall woman in a nice but comfortable-looking pantsuit. Her skin was the same rich, dark brown as Dayzha's, and her hair was a striking silvery gray. I caught myself staring at it and moved my eyes to the rest of the group instead.

Miss Chelsea's hands punctuated her sharp voice with emphatic movements. Ruth's low tones remained quiet and controlled. Mom and Dad put in a few words here and there but seemed to leave most of the talking to Ruth. As far as I could see, the newcomer didn't say anything for a while, just listened and glanced around the room with dark eyes that seemed to take everything in without judging.

The make-believe carnage seemed to have mostly died down, for which I was thankful. Kyron was now tracing dinosaur tracks while Tyrece lay on the floor helping Dayzha build an unsteady tower with the remaining specimens and Davie made occasional snapping noises and feints at them with the big T-rex. Melissa emerged from the kitchen and settled herself next to the stack of paper with the origami booklet she'd been trying to master for two weeks. Shyla had been remarkably uninvolved in the chaos, and when I glanced down at her, she was lying on the floor with her head pillowed on one arm, staring at her half-done drawing, but not making any effort to finish it or find something new.

"You okay, Shyshy?" I bent down next to her, but she suddenly rolled over with an ominous moan.

"Nan-nan, I don't feel good!"

Mom was there in a second and scooped her up while I dashed for the bucket we kept in the bathroom. When I got back, Shyla was shivering against Mom's shoulder but thankfully not sick yet. I groaned as I handed the bucket over.

"Please tell me we're not getting a stomach bug on top of everything!"

"She's not warm." Mom rubbed the little girl's back and held her close. "Shy-baby, what did you have for lunch?"

"Pizza," Shyla groaned.

"And?"

"Apple."

"And?"

"Ice cream."

"Anything else?"

"Uh-uh." Shyla shook her head, and Mom considered a moment.

"Did you have anything else to eat that wasn't for lunch?"

"Cupcakes for Jordy's birthday." Shyla's lip trembled, and Mom's eyes narrowed.

"How many cupcakes?"

"Megan didn't want hers," the little girl moaned.

"So you ate two?"

"Uh-huh."

"Shy, sweetheart." Mom sighed. "Only one dessert, remember? Ice cream or cupcake, not both. And definitely not two cupcakes. You know you feel yucky when you eat too much sweet stuff."

"I'm sorry!" Shyla wailed, and Mom turned to me with a grimace.

"See if you can find some crackers, Jen. That might settle her stomach a little."

Shyla managed a few bites of cracker before surrendering most of her lunch and her ill-fated snacks to the bucket, then leaned back against Mom's shoulder with a shuddering sigh. By the time her face was washed and the bucket emptied, she wasn't looking nearly so peaked anymore.

"Why don't you rest here for a little while, Shy?" Mom laid her on the loveseat and pulled an afghan over her. Shyla squirmed and seemed ready to protest, then stopped.

"Movie?"

Mom glanced around the room for a second, then nodded.

"Which one?"

"Strawberry Shortcake." Shyla settled contentedly against the pillows, and I fought back a laugh as I glanced at Mikyah, but he was lying with his back turned and seemed not to be paying attention. I bit my lip in sympathy as I started Shyla's movie, turning it as low as it could get without being lost in the boys' noises. Davie had apparently been inspired for a new game and was making throwing-up sounds as his dinosaur hovered over the others.

"David John." Mom's voice stopped him before I could decide whether to say something. "Not appropriate."

"Sorry." Davie ducked his head and switched back to muffled roars interspersed with strange caterwauls that sounded more like Tarzan than any living or extinct animal I could name.

While all this had been going on, the new lady had apparently been making a tour of inspection, and now she came back into the room, followed by Dad, Ruth, and Miss Chelsea. Miss Chelsea looked smug, Dad concerned, Ruth the same quietly impassive she'd appeared most of the day. The older lady walked toward the group in the middle of the floor but paused when she passed me.

"You have rather a full house here, don't you?"

I couldn't explain why, but something in her manner was relaxing, and I answered with an honesty that surprised me.

"Yeah, but I'd rather be a little crowded than lose any of the Byrd kids."

Her hand brushed lightly against my arm, but she didn't say anything as she waded into the roaring, squirming mess that was the middle of the room and crouched down. She said a few words to one or other of the kids and got quick answers as they continued with their game, not looking in the least scared or disturbed. Miss Chelsea stood near the front door eying her phone as though wondering when her boss would make the obvious decision to pack up the Byrds and leave. Mom wheeled over to where Dad and Ruth stood speaking in low tones again.

Nine

After a few minutes, the older woman stood and started back toward Miss Chelsea, but at that instant, Mom spun her chair around in a quick motion and rang the bicycle bell that was fastened to one side.

"Coming through to the couch!"

It was a rule and signal that both families had learned together when it became obvious that Mom's wheelchair wasn't able to maneuver over toys and around bodies like the rest of us could. The floor cleared instantly as the kids scrambled to their feet and pushed toys, crayons, and papers out of the way. Tyrece scooped up Dayzha, and the others faded to the edges of the room. In the sudden silence, broken only by the voices of Strawberry Shortcake's friends, I heard what Mom had somehow picked out beneath all the noise—the unmistakable wheeze in Mikyah's breathing that I'd only heard three times in the last two years, ever since Mom and Dad had been checking up on his regular medication.

"Jenna, backpack! I need his inhaler."

I heard Mom's voice through a kind of fog, and my body moved by instinct even before my mind snapped awake. Mikyah's backpack still lay where I'd dropped it in the closet. I dug through the front pocket for his emergency inhaler and ran with it to Mom. She quickly primed it, as though she'd done it all her life, and slipped an arm under Mikyah's shoulders.

"Slow, deep breath, Ky. I know it hurts, but you have to do this." She slipped the inhaler into his mouth and administered the medication, then let the canister fall and squeezed his hand tightly as he struggled to hold his breath. It should have been ten seconds; he managed five. "Dave, it's his asthma. We need to get him in to urgent care." Mom shot a glance back at Dad, who was beginning to look overwhelmed at the number of crises surrounding him.

"I'll come along, if you don't mind." The silver-haired woman spoke quietly, and Mom nodded. "Lauren, would you rather return to the office or wait for me here?"

"I'll wait here." The smug look on Miss Chelsea's face made my anger burn hot again. Mom turned to Ruth.

"Ruth, would you mind staying with Dave and the kids? Jenna, you're with me. Help me get him up. Dave, if we're not back by supper, there's some grilled chicken in the fridge and hamburger buns in the pantry. Make sure Shyla eats light."

"Is Ky gonna be okay?"

I had managed to pull Mikyah to his feet and brace myself under his weight when Tyrece's question stopped me, and turning, I saw tears in the younger boy's eyes. I didn't know what to tell him, but Mom spoke before I had to.

"He'll be all right, Rece. The doctors know what to do to help. We just need to get him there."

Dad came forward then and put an arm around Tyrece's shoulder, and Tyrece turned and buried his face in Dad's shirt. I helped Mikyah out to the minivan as fast as I could, feeling each of his wheezing breaths as he leaned against my shoulder. Mom was in her seat with her chair loaded almost before we made it.

As I watched Mikyah's labored breathing, tears flooded my eyes. Why did it have to be today—the day of all others when we needed to make a good impression and prove ourselves capable of looking out for the kids who were like second family to us? Why had Davie chosen today to start playing disgusting games with the dinosaurs? Why did Shyla have to pick today to forget her dessert rules? And why on earth did Mikyah's asthma have to flare up today when he hadn't had even a small attack in over six months? If there had been any chance of convincing Miss Chelsea's supervisor that the kids should be left with us, it was surely gone now. I buried my face in my arm and let the tears come.

Thankfully, the urgent care place wasn't far from our house, and when we reached it, I quickly dried my eyes and helped Mikyah in and over to the sick side of the waiting room, while Mom signed in at the front desk. The silver-haired social worker whose name I still hadn't gotten was only a minute behind us and sat down in a chair on Mikyah's other side. After a few minutes, Mom joined us.

"Do I need to take temporary custody for the paperwork, or do they count it an emergency?" the older woman asked, and Mom shook her head.

"It might count as an emergency, but it doesn't matter. Annetta signed medical consent forms for the kids a couple years ago so David and I could take them in if something happened while she was working." A shadow crossed her face at the last word, as if she wondered how many times Ms. B had really been working when she was supposed to be.

"Very wise." The silver-haired lady didn't comment further, and no one else spoke until we were called back. The doctor frowned as he listened to Mikyah's lungs and ordered a breathing treatment and a flu test. No one was surprised when it came back positive.

"The asthma makes him high risk. He should've had a flu shot." The doctor glared at Mom like she was somehow responsible for the fact that he hadn't, but she only nodded. He wrote out a prescription for something that was supposed to lessen the symptoms, then explained to us how to adjust his regular asthma medicine to compensate for the increased strain on his lungs. He gave us a list of the warning signs that meant we needed to get him to the hospital, although I recognized most of them from years ago when I'd first studied up on asthma. Then he dismissed us with another sour look, and we made our way slowly back to the parking lot.

Mikyah's breathing was less labored, but he still leaned hard on me, and when we reached the minivan, he dropped into the seat like he just wanted to sleep for a month. The sidewalk ramp was on our side of the van, and as I climbed into the back, the older lady motioned for Mom to wait. I paused in my reach for the handle, knowing I was eavesdropping, but not caring as much as I should have.

"Mrs. Denton?"

Mom's shoulders slumped a little as she turned back.

"Yes, Mrs. Houston."

"I realize your home is not fully equipped for a family of twelve. However, in light of the trauma the children have already sustained and the fact of your impending move, I agree that they should remain where they are at present."

"You…" Mom's voice trailed off, and she stared at Mrs. Houston in shock.

"Understand, this is not an official endorsement, Mrs. Denton. Your case will need to proceed through the courts, likely pending a home study by the Sacramento office. But I see no reason to remove the children from your temporary custody until a final decision has been made."

"After…" Mom's voice faltered. "After all this?" She laid her head in her hand and groaned. "Oh, Ruth would have my head for that!"

Mrs. Houston smiled, possibly the nicest expression I'd ever seen on anyone.

"Shall I tell you what I saw tonight, Mrs. Denton? I saw a mother able to identify a child in distress from ten feet away across a crowded, noisy room. I saw children who have adapted without complaint to a special set of circumstances and who obey without argument when it's most necessary. I saw a family willing to risk personal comfort, the judgment of outsiders, and possible legal action to do what they thought best for a family of children with no blood ties to them. Temporary crowding, messy floors, and seasonal illness do not erase that." She paused, and I thought I caught a twinkle in her eye when she went on. "May I assume that Mikyah will receive a flu shot as soon as it's offered next year?"

"He will. We all will. In fact, we'll be getting them this year." Mom straightened her shoulders and raised her head, and Mrs. Houston nodded approval.

"Now, I believe you have a prescription to fill. And I need to call off my bulldog." She pulled out her phone as she turned away, then looked back at Mom. "Lauren is young and passionate. With time and experience, she will learn. And children's lives will be better because of her."

"I understand." Mom's voice was soft. Mrs. Houston hesitated a second, then drew a business card out of her pocket.

"You understand that my recommendation is unofficial. But should you need a reference for any reason, you may call on me." She took out a pen and wrote something on the back of the card before handing it to Mom. "And it so happens that my brother is a realtor in Sacramento. If you should have trouble finding a house to fit you all, he may be able to help."

"I don't know how to thank you, Mrs. Houston." I was very sure I heard tears in Mom's voice now. Mrs. Houston smiled again.

"Go home and take care of your children, Mrs. Denton. There's nothing I'd rather have."

"God bless you." Mom barely breathed the words. Mrs. Houston lifted a hand in farewell, and as Mom wheeled around to the other side of the van, the older lady raised her head and looked into my eyes, and I realized she'd known I was listening the whole time. She turned toward her car, but not before I'd caught the twinkle in her eyes again. I smiled for what felt like the first time in hours and hurried to shut the door. When Mom had strapped herself in and put the car in gear, she looked down at the card sitting in the console and drew a long breath.

"Sheri Houston. Director of the city office." The words were spoken in a whisper, but Mikyah's eyes flickered open.

"What—what does that mean?"

Mom was silent for a minute before her soft voice drifted over to us.

"It means, Ky, that I think God's just given us our miracle." We stopped at the edge of the parking lot, and Mom reached over to grip Mikyah's hand. I laid my hand on top of hers, and she smiled. "And just maybe, He's given us—our family."

Publisher's Cataloging-in-Publication data

Names: Thompson, Angie, author.

Title: Second Family / by Angie Thompson.

Description: Lynchburg, Virginia : Quiet Waters Press, 2019. | Summary: When her best friend Mikyah and his siblings are threatened with separation, Jenna tries to help her parents prove that the Byrd children belong in their family.

Identifiers: ISBN 9781951001001 (softcover) | ISBN 9780999614495 (epub)

Subjects: LCSH: Friendship–Juvenile fiction. | Families–Juvenile fiction. | Adoption–Juvenile fiction. | BISAC: YOUNG ADULT FICTION / Religious / Christian / General.

Classification: LCC PS3620.H649 S43 2019

Made in the USA
Columbia, SC
24 September 2022